The WOMBLES

Buggy Trouble

Adapted by Elisabeth Beresford

from the Wombles television series produced by CINAR and UFTP

Hodder
Children's
Books

a division of Hodder Headline plc

"Dear oh dear," said Great Uncle Bulgaria, "what's the burrow buggy doing out here? I think I'd better move it before some human being sees it. Now I wonder how you drive it . . ."

He climbed into the buggy and tried to get it going. Suddenly, it shot forward making strange 'pop pop' noises.

What Great Uncle Bulgaria didn't know was that Tobermory and Wellington had been working underneath the buggy.

"Hey, come back!" shouted Tobermory. "I haven't finished mending the brakes yet. You won't be able to stop!"

But the buggy was making so much noise that Great Uncle Bulgaria didn't hear a word.

Meanwhile, Madame Cholet and Alderney were getting everything ready for a wonderful picnic.

"Perfection!" said Madame Cholet. "I just hope that Great Uncle Bulgaria won't be late."

"It almost looks too good to eat," said Alderney.

"Ah! Here comes Great Uncle Bulgaria," said Madame Cholet.
"But why is he driving the buggy? And he's going so fast!"

Great Uncle Bulgaria and the buggy zoomed straight through the picnic and then off again. Madame Cholet and Alderney had to jump out of the way. The food had gone flying in all directions and the picnic was ruined.

"What's going on, Tobermory?" Alderney asked him as he chased the buggy.

"The burrow buggy has run away with Great Uncle Bulgaria - and it has no brakes!"

"Oh la la!" said Madame Cholet. "We must save him!"

Over by the lake, Bungo and Tomsk were hard at work tidying up all the fallen leaves. Well, Tomsk was working and Bungo was bossing him about in his usual way.

"Hold on a minute," said Tomsk, "you're supposed to be helping, too, you know!"

"Look out!" shouted Bungo.

Great Uncle Bulgaria was zooming straight towards them - and the carefully tidied leaves. They shot up into the air and then floated down all over the place.

"Now we'll *both* have to tidy up, or the job won't be finished in time for the picnic," said Tomsk.

Tobermory had decided that the only way to help Great Uncle Bulgaria was by using the Womcopter.

"This is what we need," said Wellington as he dived into the cupboard and came out with a rope ladder.

"Well done, young Wellington. Off we go then!" said Tobermory.

Tobermory and Wellington flew high above the Common in the Womcopter looking for Great Uncle Bulgaria and then, through a gap in the clouds, they saw him far below.

"Where's he going *now*?" said Tobermory. "It looks as if that steering wheel isn't working properly. He's heading for the lake!"

The Womcopter dived down over the zig-zagging
buggy. Wellington lowered the rope ladder
and climbed down to the rescue. Somehow
he managed to open the bonnet of the buggy.

Wellington was just getting down to work when the wind caught
hold of his scarf and wrapped it round Great Uncle Bulgaria.

"Oh dear, the nights are drawing in
rather fast these days . . ." said the old Womble.
"Wellington, we're losing power,"
called Tobermory. "We'll have to leave
the buggy and land quickly!"

While all this was going on Madame Cholet had been very busy mixing an enormous cake. She took a bucket full of cake mix and got on to Alderney's skootboard. They raced after Great Uncle Bulgaria and the buggy.

"Here's my special cake for you, Great Uncle Bulgaria!" shouted Madame Cholet, and tipped the cake mix into the engine.

"Is this the right time for cake?" asked Great Uncle Bulgaria.

The engine gurgled - and a mountain of cake rose from the bonnet. The buggy stopped, right on the edge of the lake.

"It worked perfectly," said Madame Cholet. The cake was well and truly baked and the Wombles settled down for a delicious picnic.

"Thank you, Madame Cholet. I think it's the best cake I've ever tasted!" said Orinoco.

"What a very interesting day," said Great Uncle Bulgaria. "Anyone care for a lift back to the Burrow?"

But they all wanted to walk home!

First published 1999

Photographs and original artwork,
courtesy of FilmFair Ltd.
a subsidiary of CINAR Films Inc.

Copyright © 1997 Wombles Productions Inc.
(a subsidiary of CINAR Films Inc.) and HTV Ltd.
All rights reserved.
Text copyright © 1999 Elisabeth Beresford
based on the scripts from the TV series.

The Wombles ® is a trademark of Elisabeth Beresford/FilmFair Ltd

is a registered trademark of CINAR Films Inc.

ISBN 0 340 74670 X

10 9 8 7 6 5 4 3 2 1

A catalogue record for this book
is available from the British Library.
The right of Elisabeth Beresford to be identified as the
author of this work has been asserted by her.

All rights reserved.

Printed in Hong Kong

Hodder Children's Books
a division of Hodder Headline plc
338 Euston Road, London NW1 3BH